Successories®

Great Little Book on Effective Leadership

By

Brian Tracy

CAREER PRESS
3 Tice Road, P.O. Box 687
Franklin Lakes, NJ 07417
1-800-CAREER-1; 201-848-0310 (NJ and outside U.S.)
FAX: 201-848-1727

SUCCESSORIES: GREAT LITTLE BOOK ON EFFECTIVE LEADERSHIP
Cover design by Jenmar Graphics
Typesetting by Eileen Munson
Printed in the U.S.A. by Book-mart Press

To order this title, please call toll-free 1-800-CAREER-1 (NJ and Canada: 201-848-0310) to order using VISA or MasterCard, or for further information on books from Career Press.

Library of Congress Cataloging-in-Publication Data

Tracy, Brian.
    Great little book on effective leadership / by Brian Tracy.
        p.   cm. -- (Successories)
    ISBN 1-56414-328-7 (pbk.)
    1. Leadership.   I. Title. II. Series.
HD57.7.T72   1997
658.4'092--dc21   97-37336
                                                                                                            CIP

Leadership is the ability to get extraordinary achievement from ordinary people.

<⊛>

Leaders are those who determine the *Area of Excellence* for the group.

<⊛>

All work is done by teams; the leader's output is the output of his or her team.

Develop a bias for action, a *Sense of Urgency*, to get things done.

<❀>

Fast tempo is essential for success; do it, fix it, try it!

<❀>

Lead the field! Start earlier, work harder, and stay later.

Ask yourself continually, "What can I and only I do that, if done well, will make a real difference?"

Identify your areas of strength and concentrate on those areas in which you can make a major contribution.

Simplify the task. Continually look for faster, better, easier ways to get the job done.

Practice *Creative Procrastination* with low-value tasks. Put them off indefinitely.

What is your Limiting Step? What sets the speed at which you accomplish your main goals?

"Inventory can be managed; people must be led—by example."
—Ross Perot

◄ ❁ ►

Do the unexpected. You are safer moving forward than standing still.

Clarity is the key to effective leadership. What are your goals?

❮✤❯

What are you trying to do? How are you trying to do it?

❮✤❯

Be action-oriented! Lead, follow, or get out of the way.

Concentrate your powers. Identify what you are particularly good at doing and do more of it.

◁ ✤ ▷

Flexibility in a time of great change is a vital quality of leadership.

◁ ✤ ▷

Your ability to make good decisions will determine your success as much as any other factor.

9

Get the facts! Not the apparent facts, the assumed facts, or the hoped-for facts, but the real facts.

❖

Errant assumptions lie at the root of every failure. What are yours? What if they are wrong?

❖

Trust your intuition—listen to your inner voice.

If you always do what you've always done, you'll always get what you've always got.

To achieve something you've never achieved before, you must become someone you've never been before.

Is there anyone working for you who, knowing what you now know, you wouldn't hire again?

≺ ❀ ≻

Practice *Tip-of-the-Iceberg-Thinking*. Treat every unexpected event as if it were an indication of a trend.

Follow up and follow through until the task is completed, the prize won.

≺ ✵ ≻

Face the world as it is, not as you wish it were.

≺ ✵ ≻

Focus on your strengths. What are you uniquely capable of contributing to your situation?

Once you have determined your goal, concentrate single-mindedly on one thing, the most important thing, until it is achieved.

<　❀　>

Dare to go forward. Courage is the mark of greatness in leadership.

"Men must be taught at the school of example, for they will learn at no other."
—Albert Schweitzer,
   humanitarian, Nobel prize winner

≺ ❀ ≻

Refuse to make excuses or blame others. The leader always says, "If it's to be, it's up to me."

Identify your key result areas and then dedicate yourself to becoming very good in each one of them.

Continually seek ways to increase productivity, performance, and output.

Imagine starting over. Think of reinventing yourself and your business every year.

◁✿▷

Restructure your activities continually. Regularly move resources to higher-value activities.

◁✿▷

People are your most valuable asset. Only people can be made to appreciate in value.

Become the kind of person that people would follow voluntarily, even if you had no title or position.

Everyone is in the business of customer satisfaction. Who are your customers and how are you doing?

Continually tell people how good they are and what a great job they are doing.

Be willing to abandon your old ideas if someone comes up with something new and better.

"Take arms against a sea of troubles, and in so doing, end them."
—Shakespeare

Leadership in business is ultimately expressed in financial results. Continually seek ways to increase revenues or reduce costs.

◄ ❀ ►

Leaders set high standards. Refuse to tolerate mediocrity or poor performance.

Apply the 80/20 Rule to everything you do. What are your highest-value activities?

<❖>

Superior executives amaze and delight their customers. Do you?

<❖>

Quality is what the customer says it is. How do your customers define quality?

The average person works at 50 percent or less of potential. Your job is to unleash that extra 50 percent.

The most powerful and predictable people-builders are praise and encouragement.

◄ ❀ ►

Good leaders make sure that everyone knows what is expected, every single day.

◄ ❀ ►

Do you care about *me?* Answer this question of your staff on every possible occasion.

Manage by objectives. Tell people exactly what you want them to do and then get out of their way.

<❀>

Manage by responsibility. It is a powerful way to grow people.

<❀>

Manage by exception. Only require reporting when there is a deviation from the plan.

The best leaders have a high *Consideration Factor*.
They really care about their people.

＜❀＞

Practice the philosophy of continuous improvement.
Get a little bit better every single day.

＜❀＞

Take time to listen to your people when they want
to talk. This is a real motivator.

Develop a clear vision for your organization. Where do you want to be in five years?

◄ ❀ ►

What are your values? What do you stand for? Does everyone know?

◄ ❀ ►

What is your mission? Why does your organization exist at all?

Develop the winning edge; small differences in your performance can lead to large differences in your results.

Dedicate yourself to continuous personal improvement—you are your most precious resource.

The quality of your ideas will be in direct proportion to the quantity of ideas you generate.

Failing to plan means planning to fail. What are your goals?

The best leaders are the most attentive to detail. Leave nothing to chance.

◄ ✹ ►

Superior leaders are willing to admit a mistake and cut their losses. Be willing to admit that you've changed your mind. Don't persist when the original decision turns out to be a poor one.

◄ ✹ ►

Delegate the right job to the right person at the right time, and be ready to change quickly.

Keep asking yourself, "Knowing what I now know, is there any part of my business I wouldn't start up again today if I had to do it over?"

Deploy yourself for maximum *Return on Energy*.
Focus on your strengths.

Choose your people with care. Proper selection is
95 percent of success as a leader.

The best time to let a person go is usually the first
time you think about it.

◄ ❀ ►

"You can never solve a problem with the same kind of thinking that created the problem in the first place."
—Albert Einstein

◄ ❀ ►

Management is a mental game. The better you think, the greater the results you'll achieve.

◄ ✪ ►

Ask yourself regularly, "What is the most valuable use of my time right now?"

◄ ✪ ►

Outstanding leaders have a sense of mission, a belief in themselves and the value of their work.

Empower others to perform at their best by continually reminding them how good they are and how much you believe in them.

Always focus on accomplishments rather than activities.

Why are you on the payroll? What have you specifically been hired to do?

❮❀❯

What one skill, if you developed it to a high level, would have the greatest positive impact on your career?

The functions of the executive are innovation and marketing. How much time do you spend on each?

Continually focus your energies on the one or two things that represent real pay-off opportunities.

Keep people informed. Everyone wants to know what's really going on.

"I keep six honest serving men
(They taught me all I knew);
Their names are What and Why and When
And How and Where and Who."
—Rudyard Kipling

The leader acts as though everyone is watching even when no one is watching.

The leader accepts high levels of personal responsibility for performance and results.

Leaders think and talk about the solutions. Followers think and talk about the problems.

Always choose the future over the past. What do we do now?

◄ ✦ ►

Think on paper. All highly effective executives think with pen in hand.

◄ ✦ ►

Obstacles are what you see when you take your eyes off your goals.

Once you have a clear objective, think and talk only in terms of "How?"

<🕸>

When picking people for your team, the best rule is, "Hire slowly and fire fast."

<🕸>

Fast people decisions are almost invariably *wrong* people decisions. Take your time.

Self-selection is an excellent measure. Only hire people who really want the job.

◄ ❀ ►

Be perfectly selfish when you hire somebody. Only select people you like, enjoy, and want to be around.

Write out a clear, detailed description of the ideal candidate before you begin interviewing new people.

◄ ✤ ►

Attitude and personality are as important as experience and ability. Choose wisely.

◄ ✤ ►

The only real predictor of future performance is past performance. Check references carefully.

Praise is a powerful people-builder. Catch individuals doing something right.

◀ ✵ ▶

"Feedback is the breakfast of champions."
—Ken Blanchard, management writer

◀ ✵ ▶

People need regular feedback to know how they are doing and to keep on track.

The number-one *demotivator* in the world of work is not knowing what is expected.

Set clear goals and standards for each person. What gets measured gets done.

Set deadlines and sub-deadlines for all assignments.

Delegation is not abdication—inspect what you expect.

The effective leader recognizes that she is more dependent on her people than they are on her. Walk softly.

Reinforce what you want to see repeated: What gets rewarded gets done.

<◄ ❀ ►>

Start new hires off strong. Load them with responsibilities from the first day.

<◄ ❀ ►>

Keep everyone involved. Hold regular meetings to discuss the work.

"If you don't have competitive advantage, don't compete!"
—Jack Welch, CEO General Electric Company

Leadership is the ability to get followers. Do people follow you willingly?

Practice *Golden-Rule Management* in everything you do. Manage others the way you would like to be managed.

People can do amazing things if they are well-managed and properly motivated.

Be a life-long learner. Engage in daily self-renewal.

Take excellent care of your physical health. Energy and vitality are essential to effective leadership.

"The first hour is the rudder of the day."
—Henry Ward Beecher

The two major sources of value today are time and knowledge. Find new ways every day to use them better.

The key responsibility of leadership is to think about the future. No one else can do it for you.

Intellectual capital is the most valuable of all factors of production.

◄ ❀ ►

Continuous learning is the minimum requirement for success in your field.

◄ ❀ ►

Reading one hour every day in your field will give you the edge over your competition.

Crisis is inevitable. The only thing that matters is how you deal with it when it comes.

"Circumstances do not make the man; they merely reveal him to himself."
—Epictetus, Roman philosopher

Practice *Crisis Anticipation* regularly. Think about what could possibly go wrong and then provide against it.

Think! There is no problem that is not amenable to the power of sustained thinking.

The three "C's" of leadership are Consideration, Caring, and Courtesy. Be polite to everyone.

Respect is the key determinant of high-performance leadership. How much people respect you determines how well they perform.

The value of a promise is the cost to you of keeping your word.

◄ ✦ ►

Leaders think and talk in terms of excellence. This means "Be the Best!"

◄ ✦ ►

Keep raising the bar on yourself. How can you better serve your customers today?

Your weakest important skill sets the height at which you use all your other skills.

What one factor slows the speed at which you achieve your goals? How can you alleviate this constraint?

What is your next job going to be? What additional knowledge and skills will you need to perform excellently in that position?

◁ ✿ ▷

Become computer literate. Use technology to leverage your abilities.

"The very best way to predict the future is to create it."
—Michael Kami, strategic planner

◄ ✿ ►

Your ability to set goals and make plans for their accomplishment is the *Master Skill* of leadership.

Those who do not think about the future cannot have one.

◄ ❀ ►

Whatever got you to where you are today is not enough to keep you there.

◄ ❀ ►

To earn more, you must learn more.

You can learn anything you need to learn in order to achieve any goal you can set for yourself.

There is virtually nothing you cannot accomplish if you want it long enough and badly enough, and you are willing to work hard enough.

< ❀ >

"Self-discipline is the ability to make yourself do what you should do, when you should do it, whether you feel like it or not."
—Elbert Hubbard, author and lecturer

< ❀ >

The chief distinguishing characteristic of leaders is *Intensity of Purpose*.

≺ ❀ ≻

Leaders concentrate single-mindedly on one thing —the most important thing, and they stay at it until it's complete.

Simplify, consolidate, and eliminate tasks.
Reengineer your work continuously.

◁❀▷

Leaders tap into the emotions of their people by
getting excited themselves.

◁❀▷

Leadership is more who you are than what you do.

"To thine own self be true and then, it must follow, as the night the day, thou canst not then be false to any man."
—Shakespeare

‹ ❀ ›

Integrity is the most valuable and respected quality of leadership. Always keep your word.

◄ ❀ ►

Character is the ability to follow through on a resolution long after the emotion with which it was made has passed.

◄ ❀ ►

Keep asking yourself, "What kind of a company would my company be if everyone in it was just like me?"

◄ ❀ ►

Action orientation is the mark of the superior executive.

◄ ❀ ►

There are no bad soldiers under a good general.

Managers have the ability to get results; leaders have a vision of the future.

◄ ✿ ►

The job of a leader is to assure excellent performance of the business task.

◄ ✿ ►

Your job is to be a *creator* of circumstances rather than a creature of circumstances.

Resolve to be a *master* of change rather than a victim of change.

◄ ❀ ►

"If the rate of change outside your organization is greater than the rate of change inside your organization, then the end is in sight."
—Jack Welch, CEO General Electric Company

What could you do to speed up the process of delivering products and services to your customers?

<❀>

Outsource every function and activity that can possibly be done better by someone else.

<❀>

Different people require different leadership styles at different times in their careers.

Give inexperienced staff firm direction and clear guidance.

Coach and counsel continually to build top performers.

Encourage participation and involvement from everyone in the accomplishment of complex tasks.

Delegate responsibility only to those who have demonstrated the capacity to handle it.

Take time to think and reflect. Thoughtfulness is a key quality of successful leaders.

Dare to go forward! Have you ever tried pushing a string?

You are where you are and what you are because of yourself, because of your own choices and decisions.

Benchmark your performance against your best competitors. Think how you can beat them next time.

Leaders are never satisfied; they continually strive to be better.

<><❀></>

Success can lead to complacency, and complacency is the greatest enemy of success.

<><❀></>

In a time of rapid change, standing still is the most dangerous course of action.

Your outer world is a reflection of your inner world. If you change your thinking, you change your life.

⟨❀⟩

"Any addition to the truth subtracts from it."
—Aleksandr Solzhenitsyn,
   Russian Nobel prize winning author

A weakness is often a strength inappropriately applied. Move people around from one job to the other.

Create a new position if you have a talented person with a specific skill.

Avoid the comfort zone of the low performer. Set your standards higher and higher.

◄ ✤ ►

Practice management by walking around to get timely information and feedback.

◄ ✤ ►

Be prepared to modify the task or change the individual if necessary.

Your success depends upon the whole-hearted commitment to excellence on the part of everyone who reports to you.

< ❀ >

A single person who lacks commitment can be a major source of problems in your organization.

Practice *Blue-Sky Thinking*: Imagine you could do anything. What would you do differently?

Resist reverse or upward delegation. Don't let others hand the job back to you.

Leaders are demanding task masters. They insist that the job be done right.

Decide upon your major definite purpose in life and then organize all your activities around it.

Leaders accept complete responsibility for themselves in every part of their lives.

"Never complain, never explain."
—Benjamin Disraeli, British Prime Minister

Practice being a mentor to your staff. Give them guidance to advance their careers.

◄ ❁ ►

Set an example in everything you do—everyone is watching.

◄ ❁ ►

Invest in ongoing training and development of your staff.

◁ ❋ ▷

Loyalty is one of the most valuable traits of the effective executive—to your company, your boss and your staff.

◁ ❋ ▷

High performance people are dependent on high-quality relationships with their bosses.

<⬥>

Set clear priorities on everything before you begin.

<⬥>

Create an atmosphere of openness, honesty, and straight talk around you.

Truthfulness is the real mark of integrity.

Make one person responsible for each key result area.

Dress for success. Image is very important. People judge you by the way you look on the outside.

Remember the *Law of the Excluded Alternative*:
Doing one thing means not doing something else.

⟨✾⟩

Setting priorities means setting *posteriorities* as well.
What should you be doing less of?

⟨✾⟩

Long-term potential consequences are the true
measure of priorities on every activity.

Write down clear, specific goals for each area of your life.

"If you don't know where you're going, any road will get you there."
—Thomas Carlyle, British philosopher

Identify your critical success factors—the things you absolutely, positively have to do well to be successful.

≺ ❀ ≻

Do what you love to do and commit yourself to doing it in an excellent fashion.

Your company's most valuable asset is how it is known to its customers.

<⊛>

How do your customers think about you and talk about you when you're not there?

<⊛>

Perception is reality. Everything you do affects perceptions in some way.

Only undertake what you can do in an excellent fashion. There are no prizes for average performance.

Leaders do not always make the right decisions, but they make their decisions right.

Be clear about your goals. Be flexible about the process of achieving them.

< ❁ >

Unlock your inborn creativity; always be searching for newer, better, faster ways to get the job done.

< ❁ >

Innovate continually. If it works, it's already obsolete.

Identify your unique talents and abilities. What has been most responsible for your success in life, to date?

See yourself as self-employed. Treat the company as if you owned the place.

Effective leaders begin not with themselves, but with the needs of the situation. What are they?

≺ ✿ ≻

Act boldly and unseen forces will come to your aid.

≺ ✿ ≻

To overcome fear, act as if it were impossible to fail, and it shall be.

Leaders take the time to teach junior employees how to do the job well.

❮ ✿ ❯

Management enables you to move from what you can *do* to what you can *control*.

❮ ✿ ❯

Top performing leaders accept feedback and self-correct.

Imagine no limitations on what you could do. Practice "back from the future" thinking. Project forward five years and look back.

What one thing would you dare to dream if you knew you could not fail?

Think on paper. Every minute spent in planning saves 10 minutes in execution.

Develop the mind set of peak performance. Repeat, "Back to work!" over and over again.

Always be willing to consider the possibility that you could be wrong.

"Courage is rightly considered the foremost of the virtues, for on it, all others depend."
—Winston Churchill

To discover new continents, you must be willing to lose sight of the shore.

The true test of leadership is how well you function in a crisis.

◄ ✿ ►

Your ability to solve problems and make good decisions is the true measure of your skill as a leader.

◄ ✿ ►

Leaders stay calm, cool, and collected in the face of danger and difficulty.

Analyze each situation by asking, "What is the worst possible thing that could happen?" Then make sure that it doesn't happen.

Everything counts! Everything either helps or hurts, adds up, or takes away. Nothing is neutral.

The first quality of courage is the willingness to launch with no guarantees. The second quality of courage is the ability to endure when there is no success in sight.

◄ ✣ ►

The future belongs to the risk-takers, not the comfort-seekers.

Spend 80 percent of your time focusing on the opportunities of tomorrow rather than the problems of yesterday.

Do something every day to move you toward the attainment of your major goal.

"Do the thing you fear and the death of fear is certain."
—Ralph Waldo Emerson

Everyone is afraid. The leader is the person who masters the fear and acts in spite of the fear.

To motivate others to peak performance, continually make them feel important and valuable.

‹ ❁ ›

Leaders create a work environment in which people feel terrific about themselves.

‹ ❁ ›

Practice brainstorming with your staff on a regular basis. Keep them thinking creatively about the job.

Power and influence derive from the ability to help or hurt others.

The more you help others with no expectations of reward, the more rewards you will enjoy from the most unexpected sources.

Set *Peace of Mind* as your overarching goal and organize your life around it.

◄ ❀ ►

Devote uninterrupted chunks of time to the most important people in your life.

◄ ❀ ►

Remember, it's quantity of time at home, and quality of time at work, that counts.

Avoid making decisions on matters that don't need decisions. If it is not necessary to decide, it is necessary not to decide.

Build wisdom and confidence in others by forcing them to think and decide for themselves.

"Control your destiny or someone else will."
—Jack Welch, CEO General Electric Company

<∰>

Use mindstorming regularly. Define your goal in a form of a question and write out 20 answers to it.

<∰>

All strategic planning is ultimately customer planning.

Intense result orientation is the mark of the superior executive.

< ❀ >

Review each situation by asking yourself, "What did I do right?" and then, "What would I do differently?"

The *Law of Forced Efficiency* says, "There is always enough time to do the most important things."

Everything you do involves a choice between what is more important and what is less important. Choose well.

Incompetent employees undermine your credibility, sabotage your future.

<¤>

"Dehiring" is a key part of leadership. The person who keeps an incompetent employee in place is himself incompetent.

"If you aren't fired with enthusiasm, you will be fired with enthusiasm."
—Vince Lombardi, football coach

Be willing to admit you've made a poor choice—
33 percent of employees don't work out over time.

Leaders are firm, but fair and decisive when a person doesn't work out at the job.

‹❀›

What has been responsible for your greatest successes in life to date? Find out what it is and then do more of it.

◄ ❀ ►

The leader sets the tone for the whole organization. Morale always flows from the top.

◄ ❀ ►

Leaders are innovative, entrepreneurial, and future-oriented. They focus on getting the job done.

◁ ✾ ▷

Leaders are strategic thinkers. They can see the "big picture."

Leaders are anticipatory thinkers. They consider all consequences of their behaviors before they act.

Leaders have an obsession with customer service.

Leaders never use the word "failure." They look upon setbacks as learning experiences.

◄ ❀ ►

"Temporary failure is merely an opportunity to more intelligently begin again."
—Henry Ford

The future belongs to the competent. Get good, get better, be the best!

Imagine if your business burned down and you had to walk across the street and start again, what would you do differently?

You are only as free as your well-developed alternatives; what are your options to your current course of action?

React quickly to changes in the situation. When you get new information, make new decisions.

Think before acting, then act quickly and decisively.

"If a thing is worth doing, it is worth doing badly."
—G. K. Chesterton

Anything worth doing is worth doing poorly at first, and often it's worth doing poorly several times until you master it.

Work all the time you work! Don't fool around—set an example for others.

<❀>

The keys to great victories are usually speed, surprise, and concentration. They work in business, too.

Entrepreneurial leadership requires the ability to move quickly when opportunity presents itself.

◄ ❀ ►

Speed is one of the most important qualities of leadership.

◄ ❀ ►

You are only as free as your options. Continually develop alternate courses of action.

All business success is built around competitive advantage. What is yours? What should it be? Could it be?

For maximum motivation, praise in public, appraise in private.

Life is a continuous succession of problems. Solving simple problems is what qualifies you to solve even more complex problems.

Where there is no vision, the people perish. What is your vision for yourself and your organization?

"Whatever the mind of man can conceive and believe, it can achieve."
—Napoleon Hill, success author and expert

The only limits on what you can accomplish are the limits you place on your own imagination.

◁ ✿ ▷

Your life only gets better when you do. Your staff only get better when you become a better manager. Go to work on yourself.

◁ ✿ ▷

About the author

Brian Tracy is a world authority on the development of human potential and personal effectiveness. He teaches his key ideas, methods, and techniques on peak performance to more than 100,000 people every year, showing them how to double and triple their productivity and get their lives into balance at the same time. This book contains some of the best leadership concepts ever discovered.

Other best-selling audio/video programs by Brian Tracy

▶ *Action Strategies for Personal Achievement*
(24 audios / workbook)

▶ *Universal Laws of Success & Achievement*
(8 audios / workbook)

▶ *Psychology of Achievement*
(audios / workbook)

To order call: 1-800-542-4252